WHEELCHAIR RUGBY RUSH

BY JAKE MADDOX

Text by Christopher Rathje
Illustrated by Eva Morales

STONE ARCH BOOKS
a capstone imprint

Published by Stone Arch Books, an imprint of Capstone
1710 Roe Crest Drive, North Mankato, Minnesota 56003
capstonepub.com

Library of Congress Cataloging-in-Publication Data is available on
the Library of Congress website.

ISBN: 9781669007333 (hardcover)
ISBN: 9781669007296 (paperback)
ISBN: 9781669007302 (ebook PDF)

Summary: When Robinson learns about wheelchair rugby during Super
Sports Saturday, he can't wait to try it. But then his family moves to
Alabama to help take care of his grandma after she gets hurt. Robinson's in
luck, though. His dad tells him about an organization called the Shore that
has a wheelchair rugby team. Robinson is in for quite a rush as he learns
a new sport—and some important lessons about life.

Designer: Sarah Bennett

TABLE OF CONTENTS

CHAPTER ONE

UP AND AT 'EM

Is it time yet? Robinson wondered as he woke up. He looked at his alarm clock.

How can it only be 6:00 a.m.? he thought. *I'm too excited to go back to sleep!*

It was Super Sports Saturday. This was the day Robinson had been waiting for all month. His mom and dad had finally agreed to let him join the group last month. It was nice to be able to play sports with other kids with physical disabilities. And no one would tell him to slow down or be careful today.

Still, he had a hard time keeping up with the other kids last time. *Maybe this time I'll get the hang of pushing*, he thought.

Robinson sat up in his bed. He looked up at the posters on his walls. Baseball greats stared back at him—Jackie Robinson, Babe Ruth, Hank Aaron, Willie Mays, Ted Williams.

He looked at his alarm clock again—6:01 a.m. *Was time slowing down?* Waiting until 6:30 a.m. felt like it would take forever. Robinson opened and closed his hands quickly—and then again. He did that sometimes when he was really excited—or nervous. It helped him calm down. *It's not that much longer*, he thought.

Robinson glanced at the framed photo next to his clock. It was a picture of him and his family—Mom, Dad, Grandma, and Grandpa. He smiled. He loved his family. They were really supportive.

Robinson decided not to wait for his alarm to go off. He got out of bed and into his wheelchair. He headed into the bathroom and got ready for the day.

When he got to the kitchen for breakfast, his dad was sipping coffee and reading the news on his tablet.

"Man, oh man! Look at you! Someone is ready to go today!" said his dad.

"Yeah, I can't wait to get to Super Sports Saturday! I wish I could play sports *every* day," Robinson said.

Robinson began to think about all the times he'd tried playing basketball with the other kids in the neighborhood. The other kids on his team would complain that he moved too slowly. Or they'd say that his shots were too easy for the other team to block. Then, there was the time Shawn knocked Robinson over in his chair.

His parents freaked out that day. So much so that Robinson worried they'd never let him play sports again. But Robinson was fine. His parents just worried too much.

"Ready to go in twenty, son?" his dad asked.

"Yes, sir! I'll be ready to go."

CHAPTER TWO

SUPER SPORTS SATURDAY

The drive to the gym for Super Sports Saturday was short. When Robinson got inside, he saw the other kids zipping themselves around the edges of the basketball court in their track chairs.

To play almost any sport in a wheelchair, you had to be able to push yourself pretty quickly. And it wasn't as easy as it looked. You needed a strong upper body. And you had to have good coordination and quick reflexes.

Robinson smiled. He couldn't wait to get into a track chair and join them.

He found his assigned chair against the wall. It wasn't like his regular wheelchair. It had two large wheels in the back, and one smaller wheel that stretched way out in front.

Robinson got into the chair. He began strapping his legs in. He tried to strap his legs back so that they would not kick out as he pushed. Unlike most of his friends, Robinson had full feeling in his legs. He couldn't bend them in the same way they could. It was too uncomfortable. He had to strap his legs differently.

It made him feel clumsy—that and the fact that he didn't push as well as the other kids. His coordination wasn't as good. And he got tired quickly.

When he finished strapping in, he wheeled over to the other kids on the court. Coach Bee noticed him and gave him a tiny smile.

Robinson let out a heavy sigh. Coach Bee hadn't said much to Robinson since he'd joined. Robinson felt he had somehow disappointed Coach Bee already—but he wasn't sure why.

Robinson took a deep breath. *Just go out there and play with your friends.*

Robinson started pushing himself around the court. He had to push and push to gain some speed. The faster he went, the more excited he got. But before he could finish a lap around the court, his arm muscles started to burn.

He moved to the inside of the court and stopped. *How am I going to play any sport well if I don't have the strength to push right?*

A few minutes passed. The burning eased up. *Try it again, Robinson,* he thought. He started to move back toward the other kids. Then, he heard Coach Bee blow his whistle.

That meant it was time to stop. Robinson felt a little relieved. He was embarrassed that he couldn't keep up.

After everyone was back in their everyday chairs, Coach Bee gathered them around a TV in a meeting room.

"I wanted to show you all some highlights from the Paralympics. We'll be playing some of these sports soon," Coach Bee said. "Does anyone already have a favorite Paralympics sport?"

"I like wheelchair basketball a lot," said Theo.

"I like handcycling," said Luna, who was sitting right next to Robinson. "Handcycles can go even faster than track chairs!" she said with a big grin.

It made Robinson smile too. Luna *really* liked handcycling.

Coach Bee pressed play.

Blind athletes slammed themselves onto the ground to stop the ball in goalball. Wheelchair basketball players hit deep three-pointers. Tennis players lunged for the ball. It was incredible. Robinson wanted to play like that.

Then Robinson saw a game he didn't recognize. Guys and girls were in these chairs that looked like something out of a science-fiction movie. Some were smooth. They looked like they could glide through space. Others had pieces of metal that stuck out from the front. They could definitely give aliens some trouble.

Robinson studied the players as they jammed up their chairs and passed around a large ball. His eyes darted across the screen as he tried to follow their quick movements.

He watched as one player in a green jersey got loose. The player zoomed toward the other end of the court.

A player on the other team raced at him. But he couldn't get in front of the green jersey's chair quickly enough to stop him. The guy in green scraped by him. But it was so close that their wheels made a loud screeching noise.

Then, the green jersey stopped pushing. He glided through this big rectangle at the end of the court. He grabbed his wheels to stop and spun around. Then—grinning—he pumped the ball in the air.

Ha! Robinson thought. *He scored! What a rush!* He needed to know more about this game.

Robinson heard the announcer call it wheelchair rugby. He'd heard of rugby, but not wheelchair rugby. Coach Bee did say that they'd be playing these games in the future. Maybe Robinson would get to try it next month. He couldn't wait.

CHAPTER THREE

FAMILY MEETING

The next day Robinson woke up smiling ear to ear. All night he'd dreamed of playing wheelchair rugby in the Paralympics.

Robinson wasn't normally the kind of kid who got his hopes up too high. Most of the time, when Robinson tried something new, people focused on what he couldn't do.

That's what happened when he'd tried playing basketball with the neighborhood kids. His mom had watched nervously from the kitchen window every time. And when Shawn knocked his chair over, she panicked.

She ran across the street to help before Robinson could even blink. It's not like he hadn't had to get back into his chair after a fall before. And the other kids would've helped him. But his mom always overreacted.

"Robinson, I know you want to play basketball with the other kids," she had said as she helped him back into his chair. She pushed him toward the house. "But it's not the same for you. You're gonna get hurt out there."

But Robinson decided wheelchair rugby was going to be different for him. It was exactly the sort of challenge he craved—the sort of challenge he needed.

First, though, he had to know more about the sport. He got on his computer and started his research. He found plenty of websites and videos about wheelchair rugby.

Robinson learned that each team has four players. The court is a regular basketball court. And those rectangles marked off at the ends are called the keys.

The point of the game is to get to the opposite end of the court, move through the key, and cross the end line. You have to get at least two wheels over the line while holding the ball. The ball used for the game is a special volleyball. And the players use tape and glue to help them grip it.

Robinson watched a few videos. He stared in awe as the players rammed their chairs into one another. Those were hits. They maneuvered their chairs to get in the way of offensive players. They threw quick passes to their teammates. And they feverishly pushed their chairs to get past defensive players.

Robinson figured they must be really tired by the end of the game.

I don't think I could keep up. I can't even push that well, he thought to himself. He started to feel overwhelmed. *Okay. Take a breath . . . .* He decided to turn off his computer for a while.

He picked up one of his books about Jackie Robinson. He had about a dozen of them. His parents loved the baseball legend so much they'd even named their son after him.

Robinson was proud to have the famous player's name, but it felt like a lot of pressure. Jackie was such a great athlete. And Robinson wasn't—at least not yet. He worried he'd never live up to the name— especially not if his mom came running every time he took a fall or a hit.

"Family meeting, son!" Robinson heard his mom yell.

"Okay!" Robinson replied.

What could that be about? he wondered.

They only had family meetings when there was BIG news. *Was it good or bad news?*

Robinson pushed to the kitchen table where his mom and dad were already sitting. Robinson kept quiet. He waited for them to speak.

His dad began. "Son, Grandma has fallen and hurt herself. It's a pretty bad injury. Mom is going to go down to Alabama next week to help her. We're going to join her in a couple weeks. Permanently."

Robinson stared at his dad, not quite understanding.

"We're *moving* to Alabama," his dad confirmed. It's something your mom and I have been thinking about for a while. Now seems like the right time."

Robinson blinked. *They were moving to Alabama? What about his school? What about his friends?*

Then, he realized there would be no more Super Sports Saturdays. And no wheelchair rugby.

CHAPTER FOUR

THE BEST DRIVE

Two weeks went by in a flash.

As Robinson finished packing up his room,
he wondered what his new life in Alabama
would be like. His mom had *finally* begun to
let him play more sports—thanks to Super
Sports Saturday. And Robinson had even
started to make some new friends there.
Now, he'd have to start all over.

What if there wasn't anything like Super
Sports Saturday in Alabama? Robinson
started to feel really nervous. He flexed his
hands quickly.

It will be okay, Robinson, he tried to tell himself.

Robinson and his dad packed up their minivan and headed south. Robinson sat in the front passenger seat. His eyes were glued to his dad's phone, watching videos of wheelchair rugby games. It took his mind off all the uncertainty ahead.

"Ready for a new adventure?" asked his dad.

Robinson shrugged. "I don't know, Dad. I really wanted to keep going to Super Sports Saturday. And Theo and Luna seemed really cool. I won't get to play sports with them now."

"I know it can be hard to do new things. But look how joining Super Sports Saturday turned out. It'll be fine—I promise," said his dad. He reached over to squeeze Robinson's shoulder.

Robinson made a face. He went back to watching videos.

"Actually, I've been doing some research," his dad continued. "I found a place called the Shore in Birmingham. You can try all kinds of adaptive sports. Best of all, they have a wheelchair rugby team." He glanced at Robinson to see how he'd respond.

Robinson looked at his dad and broke into a huge smile. "You've been holding out on me, Dad!"

Robinson was going to get a chance to play wheelchair rugby after all. It didn't change the fact that he was leaving everything he ever knew behind—but it was something.

Robinson's dad laughed.

"I'm so excited right now! I don't even know what to think!" Robinson shouted.

Robinson still wasn't sure how he felt about the move to Alabama. But now he knew one thing for sure—he couldn't wait to see the Shore. Would the people there like him? Would he fit in? Were there other kids his age? Would someone show him how to push the right way—so that he didn't get tired so quickly? He hoped so.

I can do this, he thought.

CHAPTER FIVE

WELCOME TO THE SHORE

A week after moving to Birmingham, Robinson's parents finally took him to see the Shore.

"I'm so ready to see this place! Thanks for taking me," Robinson said.

"Sure thing, son," Robinson's dad said as they pulled into the parking lot.

As they headed toward the building, Robinson started to feel super nervous. He really wanted to play wheelchair rugby, so he wanted to make a good impression.

He hoped no one would notice how much he was sweating.

"There's the woman I met when I came the other day. Let me introduce you," said Robinson's mom once they were inside.

They approached a young woman with a sporty haircut, a muscular upper body, and a big smile.

"Hi, Sam! This is my son Robinson, who I was telling you about," his mom said.

"Hi, Robinson! I'm Sam. I work here at the Shore. And I play on the wheelchair rugby team," she said.

"Nice to meet you, Sam," said Robinson.

He didn't want Sam to think that he was a dork, so he did his best to give Sam a good handshake. But it happened so fast he wasn't quite ready.

His hand spasmed, and he missed Sam's hand at first. It required a second attempt.

Robinson's muscle spasms were something that always made him feel self-conscious about his disability. But it didn't seem to bother Sam at all. She just shook Robinson's hand and smiled.

"I'd really like to play wheelchair rugby," Robinson explained. "I just learned about it a few weeks ago. It looks so cool! I've got a million questions!" he said excitedly.

Sam laughed. "Wow, a million questions sure sounds like a lot! How about we go on the tour first? I promise I'll answer all your questions later. We'd love to have you on the team."

"The Shore is a big place, but from talking with your mom some, I have a pretty good guess what you would like to see first. Let's go to the field house," said Sam.

She was right. Robinson thought the field house was incredible.

It had three full basketball courts surrounded by a 200-meter track. And the basketball courts were lined for wheelchair rugby games! Robinson nearly burst when he saw them.

"Wait until you see the equipment closet!" Sam exclaimed. She went over to a huge set of doors and opened them. She waved Robinson over.

Robinson was overwhelmed. There were dozens—dozens!—of wheelchairs in different colors and sizes for all kinds of sports. Robinson had never seen anything like it. The Shore was his new favorite place.

"I'll arrange a time for you to meet Coach Tim real soon," said Sam. "He can get you set up with one of the rugby chairs. He'll put you through some drills before your first practice with the team. You're in for an adventure. I think you are going to love it."

CHAPTER SIX

LEARNING TO PUSH

The next day, Robinson's mom picked him up from his new school and took him to the Shore. Robinson wiggled with excitement during the drive.

"You know I'm a bit nervous about letting you play, Robinson," his mom said. "But I know you really want this, so I'm going to support you. I've also met with the coaches and drilled them about safety issues. I probably really annoyed them!" She laughed and winked at Robinson.

"Thanks, Mom," Robinson replied.

As they pulled up to the building, a man with a huge smile was waiting at the door. Robinson hoped that was Coach Tim.

"There's Coach Tim!" his mom said.

Robinson smiled back at him.

"Hi, Coach Tim!" said Robinson's mom as they approached. "Thank you for taking the time to show Robinson how to play wheelchair rugby."

"No problem!" Coach Tim replied. "This is the best part of my job—helping young people discover new possibilities. It really shows them what they're capable of."

"Sounds great," Robinson's mom replied. "Robinson, I'll be back to get you in a couple of hours. Just promise you'll be careful!"

Robinson nodded and waved at her, hoping she'd get the message. He was ready to play.

"Let's get started!" Coach Tim said.

They headed toward the field house. "We'll eventually get you hooked up with a rugby chair. But first, I'd like to just play catch for a while."

Robinson and Coach Tim traded dozens of passes. Learning passes was important because the rules of the game said players must dribble or pass the ball within 10 seconds of receiving it.

Even though Robinson was nervous, he surprised himself by catching most of the balls bounced or thrown his way. Robinson enjoyed catching the ball, but it was really dirty. Coach Tim explained that it was residue from the tape and glue players used to help them catch the ball.

Coach Tim asked Robinson to throw a baseball pass. You held the ball behind you and then threw it with one hand, like a pitcher.

Robinson didn't like it. He couldn't really control the ball that way. Some of his passes missed Coach Tim—by a lot.

Coach Tim noticed Robinson was frowning a bit. "It's okay Robinson—you've got this," said Coach Tim. "We'll just keep practicing."

Robinson saw Sam approaching. She was pushing one of the Shore's rugby chairs toward Robinson. It was a smooth offensive chair, but it looked a little big for Robinson. And it wasn't as shiny as the ones he'd seen in the Paralympic videos.

Sam placed it next to Robinson and said, "Ready to give this dream machine a whirl?"

Robinson got into the rugby chair. Right away, he loved it. "I think I'm going to like this," Robinson said to Coach Tim and Sam with a big smile.

"So, what's the best way to push it?" he asked. "I've never been very good at pushing.

I get tired before I get enough speed. But I really want to get better."

As great as it felt to sit in the cool rugby chair, Robinson still felt anxious. What if he wasn't any good? He opened and closed his hands. Once. Twice. His heart was pounding.

"Take a deep breath my friend. To learn any skill, it takes time," Coach Tim said. "The best way to learn to push is to take it nice and slow. I want you to take nice, long strokes on the wheel."

Coach Tim showed Robinson how to make long pushes while moving very slowly.

"The more you practice, the faster you'll get," he said.

Then, Sam showed Robinson the best way to play defense.

"Wheelchair rugby is known for its big hits, but I want you to focus on getting wheel position on your opponents instead," she said.

"Get your big wheel in front of my big wheel." She helped maneuver Robinson's wheel in front of hers.

"See?" she said. "If you can get wheel position, that's better than getting a hit. You've blocked me, and I can't get to the key to score."

Before Robinson knew it, he had learned the basics from Coach Tim and Sam. Next time, he would join the rest of the team for their regular practice. He had been waiting for this opportunity. He just hoped he was ready.

CHAPTER SEVEN

ROBINSON'S FIRST PRACTICE

Robinson had his mom drop him off early for his first practice with the team. The field house slowly filled up with wheelchair rugby players. The sounds of tape tearing, straps tightening, and metal wheelchairs clanking filled the air.

Robinson felt intimidated. He could see right away that he was the youngest member of the team.

His muscles spasmed as he pushed himself along the length of the basketball court to calm his nerves.

A guy who looked to be in his twenties wheeled up to Robinson and held out his hand. "Nice to meet you, Robinson. I'm Charlie. We're glad to have you."

Robinson stared at him. He knew who Charlie was. He recognized him from wheelchair rugby videos he'd seen online. Charlie was a legend. He was one of the best low-point players in wheelchair rugby.

Low-point players are usually the smartest ones on the court. They have to predict where an offensive player might go next. And then they push to get ahead of them.

"Wow!" Robinson said. Then he regained his senses and added, "Nice to meet you. I'm a big fan."

Charlie smiled and said, "Let's play!"

Practice started with some passing. Robinson learned quickly that it was important to call out names when throwing passes.

"Sam!" Robinson yelled when he threw her a baseball pass.

"Charlie—coming at you!" he called out when he sent a bounce pass toward him.

Then they did some conditioning drills. The team pushed their heavy chairs around the track. "Robinson, I'm on your right, and I'm about to pass you," Sam said as she whizzed past him.

Robinson was both impressed and discouraged. Would he ever be able to keep up with these amazing players?

Next, it was time for a scrimmage. Robinson's nerves were starting to ratchet up again.

The first time he got a clear path with the ball, he moved too close to the sideline. Next thing he knew, he was knocked out of bounds by a player on the other team. Robinson got frustrated. He felt his face turning red.

"You got the next one," said Charlie, trying to encourage Robinson. "Keep pushing—we all make mistakes."

Robinson got a nice bounce pass from Sam. Then, he turned as quickly as he could, made five strong pushes, and wheeled through the key and past the end line. He'd scored his first goal! He felt like a superhero when Coach Tim blew his whistle. Robinson let out a loud, "Woo-hoo!"

"Good job, Robby boy!" said Charlie as Coach Tim and Sam cheered.

Robinson couldn't remember a time when he had had more fun. He left the Shore with a big smile on his face.

CHAPTER EIGHT

PRACTICE MAKES PERFECT

Robinson's third practice with the team was pretty rough. He kept letting offensive players get by him because his turns weren't sharp enough. With flat turns, the offensive players were able to get better angles and get past Robinson.

Get good wheel position, he thought to himself. His frustration was building, and Coach Tim could see it in his face. He came over to talk with Robinson.

"It's okay to make mistakes, but you can't let them rattle you," he said.

"Okay, Coach," Robinson replied. He flexed his hands and took a couple of deep breaths.

Robinson tried to follow Coach Tim's advice. During the passing drills, if he missed, he told himself, *You can do this. Stay calm.* But it didn't work. He was barely catching any passes at all. He didn't know what to do.

Finally, Coach Tim blew the whistle to end practice. Charlie headed over to Robinson.

"Robby, I can tell you're frustrated. It's okay to make mistakes when you're a new player, but I have a feeling that you don't want me to give you an excuse. You want to get better."

"You're right, Charlie. I do want to get better. Sometimes I feel like I'm making progress, and other days it feels like I'm actually getting worse," Robinson confessed.

"You know what makes you better in any pursuit? Practice!" Charlie said. "I didn't just show up and win a bunch of awards. I had to dedicate myself, and I kept getting better and better. I bet if you really commit yourself, you will be amazed what you can do."

"Right. Yes. Of course. I really want to get better. Thanks," Robinson replied. He felt embarrassed that he hadn't thought of that himself. Had he thought he was just going to magically become a pro? How could he get better without more court time?

When he got home after practice, he talked to his parents about going to the Shore to practice more after school.

"I'll finish all my homework first—before any extra practices," he promised.

"You got a deal, Robinson," said his dad. "I'll take you to the Shore to practice any day you want."

Robinson started his extra practices the very next day. He came up with his own set of drills.

First, he threw the ball against the wall and tried to catch it. He would see how many times he could do that without dropping it.

Then, he pushed around the indoor track with a stopwatch around his neck. He timed each lap and kept trying to beat his record.

About a week after Robinson started his extra practices, Sam stopped by the field house to see how he was doing.

"I've heard about your new training habits," she said as she bounced a rugby ball next to her chair. "Somebody is working hard in the laboratory of life!"

Robinson cocked his head sideways. "What do you mean by that?" he asked.

Sam explained. "When I am working hard on my own and nobody is watching, I tell myself I'm working in the laboratory of life.

'The lab,' for short. It's just something I say to keep myself motivated and have a little fun."

"I like that, Sam," Robinson replied with a smile. "I might have to steal it."

"Please do!" she said. "Well, I just wanted to pop in and check on you. I'll leave you to it." She started toward the door.

"See ya later, Sam," Robinson said as he positioned himself on the track for one last lap.

* * *

For weeks Robinson practiced his wheelchair rugby skills. As he got better, playing wheelchair rugby made him feel happier.

He also felt more at home in Birmingham. Spending all that time in the field house and seeing different members of the Shore go in and out made him feel like he belonged.

One day, while finishing up his homework so that he could go to the Shore to practice, Robinson's dad stopped by his room.

"Robinson, I'm very proud of you," he said, smiling. "I can tell playing wheelchair rugby has really helped you settle in here."

"Thanks, Dad," Robinson replied. "It's helped me more than I ever imagined."

CHAPTER NINE

GAME DAY

The day of Robinson's first wheelchair rugby game had arrived. His family piled into the car with all Robinson's gear and drove to the Shore. Robinson was nervous and excited. Was he ready for this? He hoped so.

As he joined the other players, Sam looked over at him and smiled. "Everybody circle up," she said. "There's one thing we need to do before we get started."

The other players grinned as they gathered around.

"As everyone knows, we have a new member on our team—but he doesn't have a jersey yet. So let's fix that!" she said.

Charlie held up a gray jersey and presented it to Robinson.

Robinson thanked them as he took the jersey. Then he realized that the blue number on it was 42—Jackie Robinson's number. Robinson beamed with pride. He felt like he could take on the world.

"Well, let's break that jersey in, yeah?" Coach Tim said.

"Yeah!" Robinson shouted.

Robinson put on his new jersey and smiled to himself. Then, he made sure the tape was nice and snug around his gloves.

Robinson's family watched as he did warm-ups with the team. His mom was impressed by how well Robinson was pushing.

"Great job, son! Keep it up!" she exclaimed.

Robinson looked and smiled. Hearing his mom's encouragement made Robinson feel proud. But he was feeling nervous too. The Shore was playing one of their biggest rivals, Hope Center.

Charlie noticed Robinson's expression change.

"Robby boy, don't worry!" he called. "Just do your best and have fun. Get out of your head and enjoy the moment!"

Robinson perked up a little after Charlie's pep talk. He was ready to play.

Robinson started the game on the bench. He was relieved to get to watch his team in action before he had to take the court.

The Shore won the opening tip, and someone tapped the ball to Sam.

"Charlie, I need your pick!" Sam yelled.

Charlie pushed toward the Hope Center players moving toward Sam. He blocked one of them with his picker bar—the small wire basket sticking out of the front of his chair. And the other players piled up behind him.

Charlie successfully clogged up the defense, and Sam glided past them and scored the first goal of the game. The crowd erupted in applause.

"Alright, Sam!" Robinson yelled.

The rest of the first quarter went by quickly with the teams trading goals back and forth. The Shore was leading Hope Center 12–10.

Sam and Charlie continued their stellar defense during the second quarter. Twice they positioned their chairs and completely trapped Hope Center's main ball handler. He had to throw wild passes that resulted in easy turnovers.

By halftime, the Shore widened their lead to 24–17.

With a couple minutes left in the third quarter, Coach Tim told Robinson to check in at the scorer's table. He was up next!

When the ball rolled off the chair of one of the Hope Center's players and went out of bounds, Robinson was called into the game by a referee. Robinson took a deep breath and rolled onto the court.

Sam inbounded the ball, passing it to Robinson. "Look to your left, Robinson!" she yelled.

Robinson maneuvered toward the sideline, looking for an opening to push up the court.

"Use Charlie's pick!" Sam told Robinson.

Robinson got free from the Hope Center players, put together seven pushes to hit the end line, and scored his first goal. He was so excited, but he didn't have time to celebrate.

He had to get ready to play defense.

A few minutes later, Robinson got the ball again. He realized he was too close to the sideline. A player from Hope Center knocked him out of bounds.

Robinson got frustrated, and his muscles tensed up.

Stay calm, he reminded himself. He regained his focus and pushed hard to get into a good defensive position again.

When the buzzer sounded to end the third quarter, Robinson gave himself a pep talk. *It's okay. It's okay to make mistakes. Stay calm. Be in the mome*nt, he thought as he chugged cold water.

The buzzer sounded to start the fourth quarter. Coach Tim waved at Robinson to stay in the game.

Hope Center inbounded the ball to their main ball handler.

Robinson stayed about three pushes off Hope Center's low pointer to avoid being clogged up. As the ball handler separated himself, Robinson got wheel position on him.

Robinson yelled, "Sam, I'm trying to keep wheel position. I see the ball. Ball! Ball!"

Robinson stopped the ball handler in his tracks. Hope Center received a score clock violation because of Robinson's great defense.

The final quarter went by in a blur. Robinson played well on both offense and defense. Then, just as the quarter was wrapping up, Robinson caught a pass from Sam.

"Charlie, I need your block!" Robinson yelled.

Charlie delivered a great block against two Hope Center players. Robinson pushed hard toward the end line. He scored!

The crowd erupted in cheers. The final buzzer sounded.

The Shore's bench started to shout, "Forty-two! Forty-two! Forty-two!"

Sam came over and congratulated Robinson. "Great job, Robinson! I'm really proud of you! Looks like that lab work you did really paid off!"

Robinson smiled and gave her a fist bump.

Charlie added, "You did such a great job communicating out there and playing hard. Way to go, Robby boy!"

He waved with gusto at his family.

Robinson's dad and mom waved back. "Way to go, Robinson!" they screamed.

Robinson was so proud. He couldn't stop smiling. He looked over at Coach Tim, who had a big grin on his face too. Robinson wasn't sure whose smile was bigger.

When they got home, Robinson's dad put his arm around him and said, "You did a great job, son!"

"Thanks, Dad," Robinson said. He couldn't believe how different he felt from a few months ago. He had grown bigger and stronger. But he'd grown in other ways too. It was like everything about him felt a little bit more powerful.

Robinson cleaned up and went to his room. He got in bed and started thinking about what else he might do. Coach Tim had mentioned that a junior wheelchair rugby team had just started in Canada. Could he be playing with kids his own age soon? Would he keep playing wheelchair rugby until he was an adult?

Robinson decided to think about all that later. Right now, he would just enjoy the moment.

AUTHOR BIO

 Christopher Rathje discovered adaptive athletics when he was nine years old. He competed in wheelchair track and field, wheelchair basketball, and wheelchair rugby. For four years, he played wheelchair rugby with the Lakeshore Foundation in Alabama. He also volunteered to help kids play wheelchair basketball on a national level. Christopher attended the University of Illinois and Northwestern University.

ILLUSTRATOR BIO

 Eva Morales is a professional 2D illustrator and artist living in Spain near the Mediterranean Sea. She worked in children's publishing, TV, film production, and advertising for about 14 years. Now she works as a full-time freelance illustrator, using a combination of digital and traditional techniques. Eva loves to walk on the beach and read books in her spare time.

GLOSSARY

adaptive sports (uh-DAP-tiv SPORTS)—sports that have been changed so that athletes with disabilities can play them

anxious (ang-SHUHS)—feeling worried or fearful

maneuver (muh-NOO-ver)—to make planned and controlled movements that require practiced skills

Paralympics (pa-ruh-LIM-piks)—a series of international competitions for athletes with disabilities

pick (PIK)—an offensive move in which a player uses their chair to block a defensive player so that they can get someone on their team free

pursuit (pur-SOOT)—the act of trying to do or get something

push (PUSH)—using one's arms to move the wheels of a wheelchair; pushing takes the place of walking or running for a person who does not use a wheelchair

residue (REZ-uh-doo)—what is left after something is used or removed

self-conscious (self-KON-shuhs)—being too concerned with what others might think of you

DISCUSSION QUESTIONS

1. Throughout the story, Robinson gets frustrated when he's not able to keep up with others during practice. What helps him get better at playing wheelchair rugby?

2. When Robinson sees the clips of wheelchair rugby for the first time, he wants to learn as much as he can about the sport. He does a lot of research online, and he watches a lot of videos. What sport or activity have you had a strong interest in? What did you do to learn more about the sport or activity?

3. Robinson is named after baseball legend Jackie Robinson. How did being named after this athlete make him feel in the story? Do you think it's a good thing or a bad thing to be named after someone?

WRITING PROMPTS

1. Robinson flexes his hands to help himself calm down when he's excited or nervous. Write a list of things you do to help yourself calm down when you're nervous.

2. Robinson takes Charlie's advice about practicing more often so that he can play wheelchair rugby better. Write a paragraph that describes a time when practicing more helped you get better at something.

3. At the end of the story, Robinson makes some big plays during an important game for his team. What do you think will happen when he goes to the next team practice? Write the scene.

MORE ABOUT
WHEELCHAIR RUGBY

Wheelchair rugby started in the 1970s in Canada as a team sport for quadriplegics—people who have permanent physical disabilities in four limbs. In 1996, it was a demonstration sport at the Atlanta Paralympics. In 2000, it became a full medal sport at the Sydney Paralympics.

Wheelchair rugby mixes elements of rugby, basketball, ice hockey, and handball. Teams of four play against each other on a basketball court. To score a point, a player must have at least two wheels of their wheelchair cross a line at the end of the court while they have possession of the ball. The team with the most points after four eight-minute quarters wins the game.

Men and women play together on rugby teams. A classification system for the players—which is common in adaptive athletics—determines which four players are on the court together. Players are assigned a point value. It can be .5, 1.0, 1.5, 2.0, 2.5, 3.0, or 3.5. The total points for the four players on the court for a team must be less than or equal to 8.0.

MORE FROM JAKE MADDOX!

READ THEM ALL !

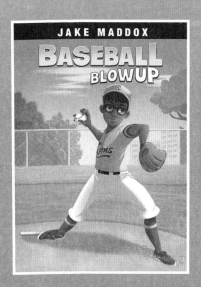

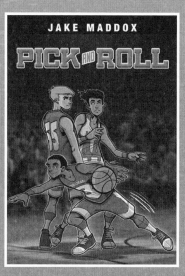

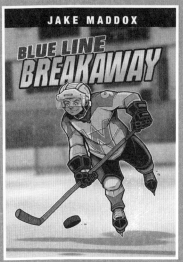